# Family Recipe

## Sweet and saucy stories, essays, and poems about family life

### Theresa Hupp

# COPYRIGHT

ISBN: 978-0-9853244-0-7

ISBN-10: 0985324406

Rickover Publishing

**Family Recipe: Sweet and saucy stories, essays, and poems about family life**

# ACKNOWLEDGEMENTS

The essay *"Normally Dysfunctional"* was previously published in ***Chicken Soup for the Soul: All in the Family*** (2009).

The short story *"Family Recipe"* was previously published in ***Kansas City Voices***, Volume 9 (Whispering Prairie Press, 2010).

My gratitude to the members of the Kansas City Writers Group and the Homer's Orphans critique group who provided input on many of these pieces, and to Write Brain Trust for advice on publishing.

And most of all, my love and appreciation to the family members mentioned in this book, whose lives are intertwined with mine in ways that bring me joy and writing material.

# CONTENTS

# NORMALLY DYSFUNCTIONAL

"At least you're not my real mother!"

My daughter's words interrupted my tirade. I was fixing dinner, worrying about work, and wondering why my husband was late getting home. Six-year-old Marcy had brought me some small problem. It was one thing too many for my frazzled brain, and I yelled at her across the kitchen island.

But her tear-filled eyes and quiet voice stopped me. "What on earth do you mean?" I asked.

"I know I'm adopted."

I stared. Was she in that phase already? For years as a child, I had wanted to be adopted, painfully embarrassed by my not-so-cool mother and father. Surely my real parents were out there, I thought, ready to sweep me away to a world where I would be pretty and popular. If only I could find them. But my desire for different parents hadn't surfaced until I was a pre-teen. At six, I hadn't worried about where I fit into the world.

And my yearning to be adopted hadn't lasted long. Once I could calculate that I was born nine months and ten days after my parents were married, and knew the significance of that timing, my dreams were dashed. I couldn't be adopted. No one in their right mind would adopt a kid that soon after marriage, particularly not a good Catholic couple, who were far more likely to have been surprised by their quick fertility than to have sought to raise someone else's child.

But that evening Marcy was serious. She thought she was adopted. I needed to set her straight.

"Marcy," I said, "I was there when you were born. Trust me, you weren't adopted. I'd know. Besides, you know people always say we look alike." Back then, she did look like me.

Marcy looked dubious. But she didn't say anything more. I never heard her mention her adopted status again, and I forgot about this incident for years.

### 

Marcy and her older brother Jamie grew into young adults. We had our ups and downs. Some undisclosed speeding tickets, some underage drinking. But they both got good grades and worked hard most of the time. Jamie did well in forensics, and Marcy in athletics. Both could hold their own in dinner-table discussions. By the time they graduated from high school, they were good company.

After they left for college, my husband and I didn't see much of them, because they went to school far away. But we enjoyed them when they returned home on breaks, which came less and less frequently.

One holiday when they were both home, the kids and I were chatting. The conversation turned to how they got along as children. I suspected there had been more sibling rivalry between them than they had disclosed when they were younger. They confirmed my suspicions.

"You know, Mom," Marcy said, "Jamie convinced me I was adopted when I was a kid."

"What?" I exclaimed.

"Yep. He said you and Dad didn't want me to know until I was older, so I wasn't supposed to say anything to you."

"You believed him?" I asked, incredulous.

"For two or three years."

I sat in shocked horror. My baby had thought she was adopted?

And then I remembered the incident when she was six.

"How could you have done that?" I asked Jamie. "Why were you so cruel?"

He just shrugged and smiled sheepishly.

We talked some more, about the awful things that family members do to each other. They mentioned friends, some of whom had serious problems with substance abuse or eating disorders, whose parents had gone through nasty divorces, or who were unable to cope with the stresses of school and peer pressure.

"I've always been grateful our family was just normally dysfunctional," Marcy said. "We may have done mean things sometimes, but we generally liked each other."

Normally dysfunctional. I raised my kids in a normally dysfunctional family. I still think that's the best compliment I've ever received as a mother.

# GIFT FROM A CHRISTMAS BEFORE MEMORY

"Baby Jesus needs a present. Why don't you give him YaYa?"

YaYa was my beloved stuffed ducky when I was a toddler, my favorite friend, my lovey. His downy fuzz so soft to my fingers during nap time, his size and weight perfect for cuddling. I had hugged and caressed him so often in our time together that his fluff had worn away to bare skin below, his beak torn off and gone.

Mommy thought he was disgusting.

That Christmas day when I was not yet three, we were at early morning Mass. Mommy whispered for me to give YaYa to Baby Jesus as a birthday present.

I nodded at her suggestion, pleased and proud to have something to give to Baby Jesus.

With one chubby hand I nestled YaYa against my chest, and I gave my other hand to Daddy. The three of us – Daddy, me, and YaYa – marched up the aisle to the beautiful crèche, sparkling with starry lights set in fragrant pine boughs beside the altar.

When we reached the front of the church, I rubbed my ducky's downy breast one last time and set him gently in the manger by Baby Jesus. Daddy and I said a little prayer.

I grinned as I raced back to the pew where Mommy sat with my baby brother.

Mommy smiled at me.

At least that's how I imagine what happened that Christmas morning. I don't remember leaving my worn-out YaYa in the crèche. I don't even remember loving YaYa. (Yet as I write, I'm convinced YaYa was a "he," not an "it" or a "she," so perhaps I have retained some vague sense of YaYa's personality, his meaning in my toddler's existence.)

Although I don't remember, I heard the story repeatedly over the years. It became one of those Christmas tales that make up family traditions. How Mommy thought my stuffed duck was filthy, its seams split and yellow cloth darkened from all my fingering. How I wouldn't even let Mommy take YaYa to wash him, but then gave my ducky to Baby Jesus without a second thought. How Daddy snuck back to the crèche after Mass and retrieved YaYa, hiding it away from me, in case I asked for him later (though I never did).

To me, the family lore about YaYa was all just a story, not a part of my maturing reality.

When I reached adolescence, I couldn't even imagine myself having a lovey, and I certainly couldn't picture YaYa. I became troubled by the tale, not amused.

I realized how my parents had manipulated me. They had taken advantage of a small child's dawning understanding of Christmas as a birthday celebration to get rid of a household nuisance. As I thought about the story, I decided the fact that Daddy retrieved the toy did redeem their subterfuge. I am sure that had I needed YaYa, he would have magically reappeared, perhaps a gift from Baby Jesus back to me.

Still, I wondered at whether my parents should have taken away their child's favorite possession.

Many years later, when my own son became attached to a beloved silken blanket, I told him – argued with him – when it needed washing, but I never tried to get him to give it up. I let him sleep with it well into grade school, when on his own he packed it into a dresser drawer (where it remains today, though he is well into adulthood).

Then a few years ago, when my parents were downsizing their home, they sent me a box of childhood mementos. In the box was YaYa.

When I saw the toy again, I still didn't recall YaYa from my childhood, though I knew immediately that this dirty, bald duck with missing beak must be YaYa – the subject of the family lore.

I decided when I saw him my mother had been right – YaYa had lived far past his prime.

And with my middle-aged perspective, I realized that perhaps being a present for Baby Jesus was the best end YaYa could have expected. After all, my parents could have stolen him away one day without telling me. They could have thrown him in the trash. At least YaYa ended his useful life by becoming a present to a baby who needed him more than I did.

Now, when I occasionally open the box containing YaYa, I put a different interpretation on the story. It's not the story of young parents – younger than my son is now – manipulating an innocent child.

It's the story of parents trying their best to raise a generous and faithful child. I may not remember that Christmas morning, but I can remember my parents through my childhood doing the best they could to raise me to be loving and giving.

# DRIVING TO DES MOINES

Connie Pearson didn't mean to run away from home. Attorneys with young children don't have time to run away.

She rushed out of her office at 5:45 Thursday afternoon. She had to get the kids by 6:00. She was late. The last day care center worker, who always had to wait for the late parents, would shake her head at Connie again. It happened at least once a week.

Connie buckled the seatbelt in her minivan, squealed out of the parking garage, sped through two yellow lights in downtown Kansas City, and wove through the freeway lanes north over the Paseo Bridge. Thank God, traffic was light. She might just make it, or at least not be the last parent to arrive. Her kids hated that.

Connie's mind drifted. Her meeting that morning hadn't gone well; the client wasn't happy. Pre-trial brief due on Monday. Argument with George last night; what had started it? Who would get the clothes at the cleaners? The dog's flaky skin was back; the medicine wasn't working. A new client wanted her to file a complex patent lawsuit. How could she get it all done?

Connie meant to take the Antioch exit after crossing the Missouri River, but she passed right by it. Damn. The car should be able to drive the route by itself.

Now the Chouteau exit loomed ahead. Still angry with herself,

Connie hit the accelerator. Just driving, fantasizing about leaving her problems behind, was exhilarating. Past Chouteau. Past Brighton, the last opportunity to get to the day care center without losing much time.

"Des Moines" read the highway sign above her head. Connie had never been to Des Moines. She'd never been to Iowa. She'd lived in Kansas City for ten years, and never been to Iowa. Vacation time went to family visits on the West Coast, except for the week-long fling she'd spent with George in Jamaica for their fifth anniversary.

Des Moines. The name was faintly exotic, but solidly grounded in the Midwest. Des Moines. She could be there by dark. No, she couldn't do that. She'd just drive to Liberty, then turn around. She'd only be fifteen minutes late to get the kids. George was often that late when he picked them up. The kids wouldn't even know.

The first exit for Liberty came into view. Connie drove on. The second Liberty exit slipped away also. She really should turn around. A semi passed her on the right, and she couldn't get over into the exit lane. She kept driving.

Connie left the suburbs behind. She opened her sunroof and breathed in deeply. The evening summer air was balmy, not too sticky for once.

She picked up her cell phone, dialed George's office number. His voice mail answered.

"George. Sorry I didn't call earlier. Didn't have a chance. Last minute problem. I'm going out of town for a client. You'll have to get the kids. See you tomorrow night. I'll call later."

Connie's stomach lurched toward her throat as she hung up. She'd never done this before. She felt guilty. She breathed the summer air again, and pushed on the gas pedal. She felt free.

Another sign beckoned "Des Moines."

Connie drove north, with the sun dropping over her left shoulder. The evening air was intoxicating, but Connie barely noticed. What had she done? Why was she doing this? Didn't she love her family?

The dog had to go to the vet on Saturday; same time as Erin's T-ball game. Could George take the dog? Or would he rather go to T-ball and the team pizza party afterwards? George hated kindergarten T-ball; "all they do is kick the dirt," he fumed. But he hated the dog, too; it was really hers. Connie kept driving.

Gradually, Connie's mind cleared. She didn't think about anything. When was the last time she hadn't had some chore to think about? She saw the cornfields waving along the road and heard the beginning of a meadowlark's riff as the car sped along. The peace was heavenly.

By the time Connie reached Cameron, the car needed gas. She stopped at a convenience store. After paying for the gasoline and a snack, she hesitated beside the driver's door. North or south? The damage was already done. She continued north.

The silence continued. She didn't want it to end.

Sooner than she expected, she was in Iowa. Iowa didn't look any different than Missouri, but it was new ground. Now she could say she'd been to Iowa. Was that enough? Should she head home? But she could be in Des Moines in another hour, still before dark on this long summer day. Connie kept driving.

What should they do about Jason's teeth? He needed braces. But if he got them now, he'd probably have metal in his mouth for six years. Like her brother had. How long could they wait to fix his overbite?

How could she get her brief filed on time? Her managing partner would be out all day Monday, and he wanted to approve it. The client was already miffed; it would have to be a great brief. Maybe they should settle the case. But how could she talk settlement when the client was mad? And how could she take on a new patent case? She'd never handled an infringement claim before.

Why on earth was she driving to Des Moines? How would she patch this up with George? Had she temporarily lost her mind? Or maybe it wasn't temporary; maybe it was the start of early Alzheimer's. Ever since Grandma died of Alzheimer's two years ago, Connie worried about every mental lapse.

Des Moines, 50 miles.

All right, she was driving to Des Moines. What would she do when she got there? She had a laptop, but no toothbrush. George would never believe she'd headed out on a business trip without her roll-on suitcase. She kept it packed for emergencies like this. What would she tell him?

The sunset streamed across the sky, clouds flashing pinks and oranges before burning to grey. When was the last time Connie had seen the sun set, at least to notice more than to call the kids in from playing in the yard? Her throat swelled. Why didn't her life let her watch sunsets anymore? She used to be good with a camera. She'd spent many evenings during college – and even law school – photographing sunsets that were different and glorious every night. Never had time any more.

Des Moines. Connie had reached the outskirts. Now what? She continued north on I-35 until she saw an exit with several hotels and restaurants. Should she eat and turn around? She'd be home about midnight; too late for an argument with George. Should she check into a hotel and figure it out in the morning? Personal credit card or law firm card? How incognito did she want to be?

Connie turned into the Wal-Mart parking lot. She hated shopping, and particularly hated Wal-Mart, but shopping would defer her decision-making, and she didn't know where else to go. She bought a toothbrush, toothpaste, deodorant, a package of underwear and a nightshirt. It looked like she was staying the night.

She headed back toward the interstate and stopped at a hotel that was part of a familiar chain. She knew what the room would look like, and they had free breakfasts. She checked in, hesitating momentarily before pulling out the firm credit card. Better safe than sorry. She could decide later what to tell George.

Connie took her laptop in its briefcase and her Wal-Mart plastic bag up to her room. She closed the hotel room door, locked it behind her, and sat down on the couch with her meager possessions beside her.

And burst into tears. What in God's name was she doing in Des Moines? Didn't she love her family? And her job; she'd worked so hard for this job. Was she throwing it all away?

Slowly her tears ended, if only because she couldn't answer the questions she asked herself. Connie breathed in the silence. She breathed deeply, and she calmed. She had one night. One night when she didn't have to worry about anyone or anything. She might as well sleep.

Connie brushed her teeth, put on her new nightshirt and got into the king size bed, relishing the space and solitude. As she plumped the five pillows to her satisfaction, she remembered she'd told George she would call.

Sighing, Connie reached for her cell phone and hit the speed dial for Home.

"Where are you?" George asked.

"Des Moines."

"What the hell are you doing there?"

"Got a new client," Connie stated. Which was true, but was not an accurate response to George's question. It was the biggest lie she'd told George in their twelve years of marriage. She was stuck now. "I've got some things to do here. I'll be home tomorrow night."

"Why didn't you let me know before 6:15?" Hell, she hadn't known she would be gone until 6:15. "The day care center was pretty upset when I waltzed in at 6:30. That's the latest we've ever been. Erin was crying."

"You're right," Connie said. "I should have called. I got caught up. I'm sorry. Tell Erin I'm sorry."

"We've got to do a better job of keeping ourselves on schedule," George said in his precise accountant's voice. "We're both in stressful jobs, with lots of demands on our time. It's not fair to the kids. You're the one who wanted kids so badly, but you're not doing your part."

Why did George always lecture her? "George, it's late. I don't want to argue. Just let me get back home. We'll talk."

"All you want to do is talk. You never want to change anything. When are you going to realize you've got to make some changes? Show this family means something to you."

"I'll see you tomorrow, George." She didn't add her usual closing of "Love you."

Connie hung up, and turned out the light. But sleep in the strange hotel room eluded her. What was she thinking, abandoning her family and lying to her husband? She threw her arm over her eyes to blot the tears. What was she going to do now?

Des Moines. The name no longer seemed exotic. Just another Midwestern city with flat horizons. She was still Connie, and her problems still loomed.

Connie drifted off to sleep, but was wide awake at 3:00am. Her deception had bought her a day; now what was she going to do with it? It was too early to do anything else, so she powered up her laptop, opened the pre-trial brief, and started typing. By 5:00am, she had completed a draft of the brief. She e-mailed it to her partner. Her message to him said she wouldn't be in the office that day due to a personal crisis, but she promised she would review any comments he e-mailed back and would get him the final brief by first thing on Monday.

Personal crisis indeed. Another lie. The only crisis was that she'd lost her mind. But at least she was keeping up with work; she should still have a job on Monday.

It was 5:00am, and the day stretched ahead. She'd need to leave Des Moines by 2:00 or 2:30, so she could pick up the kids. She had to be on time, as a sign of good faith to George. That left seven hours for her to fill.

And she still didn't know what the hell she was doing in Des Moines.

Connie showered, dressed in the same clothes as the day before, ate an early breakfast, and lingered in the small hotel dining area over her free copy of USA Today with a second cup of coffee. She negotiated with the front desk to delay her check out until 2:00. Then she went back to her room and checked her voice mail and e-mail. No new messages. What else could she do?

Wal-Mart. They open early. She could buy a blouse and socks. Off she drove to Wal-Mart. She walked through the women's clothing department and saw a rack of swimsuits marked down in a mid-season sale. She hadn't had a swimsuit on in three years. But there was a pool at the hotel, and the summer day was already hot. She took a swimsuit in her size off the rack. If it fit, fine, if it didn't, it was only $10. She bought sunscreen as well, knowing she'd get fried without it. And a long blouse and socks.

Back at the hotel, Connie checked her e-mail and voice mail again. A few new messages, but no catastrophes. She sent her responses quickly and still had half the morning left.

She looked out her window. The pool glistened blue-green. She tried on the swimsuit, which fit well enough for a pool where no one knew her. She threw on the Wal-Mart blouse over it, picked up a stack of reading from her briefcase, the hotel towel and her sunscreen, and headed to the pool. She chose a plastic lounge in the full sun, and sat down.

Connie knew she was simply filling her time with activities so she wouldn't have to think. She needed to figure out why she'd taken off for Des Moines, but she didn't have a clue. She opened her legal reading, but couldn't focus.

"Why am I in Des Moines?" she asked a sparrow hopping near her lounge.

She got no answer from the bird, and Connie had no answers herself. Her life threatened to drown her. But everyone she knew was in the same boat she was – her colleagues at work, her friends, other parents in her kids' classes. And George. Why should she feel any different from George? George never ran away.

Unless she counted his annual trip with his college roommate. Now that she thought about it, that really ticked her off. He took a week off every summer with his buddy to go to baseball games – he'd gone just last month in fact – while she stayed home with the kids and the dog and went to work. When was the last time she'd had even a weekend with a friend? The week with her parents three years ago after her mother's hysterectomy didn't count. Why did she have to lie to get a measly day in Des Moines?

Okay, she needed time away. This trip was a way of grabbing time for herself. Still, she shouldn't have lied to George. Should she tell him what she'd done? Or keep up the story about the new client? George would never know; he never asked about her cases and never talked about his auditing work.

How could she get away, when the firm demanded more billable hours every year? She could set her own hours to some degree, but the firm still expected her to bill her share of time and to be available whenever clients wanted her. Some flexibility that gave her. A long weekend meant a week or more of extra hours on either side to catch up.

And the kids' schedules confined her as well. She already got to work as early as she could after getting the kids out of bed. George drove them to school, but she had to leave work by 5:30 each night to get the kids. Evenings and weekends were spent on the kids' swimming lessons and softball, on catching up her work, and on laundry and the minimal housework she did.

The kids. Tears came to Connie's eyes again as she thought about Erin and Jason being the last ones at day care yesterday. Such good kids. She loved them completely, and wished she were a better mom. In her heart, she knew it would be harder to lose one of them than George, though she'd never tell George that. Was she going to lose them because of this crazy trip to Des Moines? The thought panicked her. But she didn't move from her lounge. She was going to eke every hour of time to herself she could. She'd do something fun with the kids when she got back.

The sun baked into Connie's skin as noon approached. She lay on the lounge trying to relax, but her mind raced, flitting from problem to problem. This wasn't doing her any good. She hadn't resolved any of her problems, and she'd added the worry of what to tell her family and office when she returned. Oh, well, she'd deal with it when the time came.

At 12:30, Connie reluctantly returned to her room. She showered again, dressed and checked voice mail and e-mail. There were a couple of Friday afternoon frenzied messages, but responses could wait until Monday – her clients just lobbed their problems to Connie so their weekends would be free. No revisions yet on the brief from her partner.

Connie shoved her purchases back into their Wal-Mart sacks and checked out of the hotel. She started her minivan, waited for the air-conditioning to chase the heat out of the car, and turned south on the freeway towards Kansas City. So much for Des Moines. Next time, she'd run away somewhere more exciting.

When Connie got home, she unloaded her briefcase and shopping bags into the kitchen, and dialed George's office. "I'm back," she said into his voice mail. "I'm getting the kids. Dinner'll be ready when you get home." She drove to the day care center and walked in, surprising Erin and Jason at the after school program.

Erin frowned at her. "Mom, you're early. I need to finish this painting."

"How pretty, sweetie," Connie said, hugging her daughter, "I thought we'd go to Penguin Park." It was a favorite playground for the kids. Erin's frown turned to a smile.

Jason, too, was at first reluctant to leave his friends. "Why are you here?" he asked.

"I'm making up for yesterday," Connie said. "Taking you to Penguin Park." Jason dropped his toys in their basket and followed her out to the van.

At the park, Jason and Erin spilled out of the car and ran shrieking toward the oversized penguin and kangaroo statues that held swings and slides. They played noisily while Connie watched, waving when one of them yelled "Watch me, Mom!"

When the kids were tired, she loaded them into the van and headed home. "That was great, Mom!" Jason said as they walked

15

into the kitchen. "Why can't we go to the park every day?"

"I can't pick you up early all the time," Connie said, pushing his sweaty hair off his forehead. "But maybe we can go more often."

Erin's hug and grin in response melted Connie's heart. Yes, she thought, they should go to the park more often.

And maybe she needed more play dates for herself as well. Maybe, just maybe, she'd find time to run away again. But next time, she'd plan it.

# JUST THE FLOWER GIRLS' AUNT

I don't have much experience with weddings, other than as a guest. I was the bride once, but after I bought my dress, all I had to do was fly in from graduate school (with groom in tow) to the festivities my perfectionist mother planned. That was fine with me. I didn't care about food or flowers or frou-frous; I had another draft of my law review note due two weeks later.

My sister Rosemary was thirteen at the time. "She's too old to be a flower girl," my mother fretted during the planning phase. "But she could be a junior bridesmaid."

"What's the difference between that and a real bridesmaid?" I asked. "Just call her a bridesmaid."

"We don't have anyone in the family the right age for a flower girl," Mother said.

"We don't need one," I said. "Keep it simple."

Later experience proved my approach was correct.

Eleven years after my wedding, I was a bridesmaid for Rosemary. My six-year-old son James was her ring bearer, and the groom's five-year-old sister the flower girl. My three-year-old daughter was most upset not to be a flower girl as well. We consoled her by naming her "Daddy's date," but without a white dress and flowers, she didn't think she had an adequate role.

Though no romances developed between bridesmaids and groomsmen that day, everyone fell a little bit in love with James in his tux and the flower girl in her blond curls. The music cued for the children to start down the aisle.

Just as I launched them, James lifted his little pillow with fake gold bands and asked, "When do I get the real rings?" I hadn't realized he would take his responsibilities so seriously.

"I'll tell you later," I said, and pushed him forward.

Between thwarting his possible tantrum, trying not to step on my poufy-sleeved floor-length pink bridesmaid dress, and consoling my peeved daughter, I had plenty of drama that day. I was glad I was never asked to be a member of a wedding party again.

I never did explain to James about the rings.

Another decade passed, and it was my brother's turn. Rosemary's daughters, Katie (age five) and Megan (age three), were the flower girls at his wedding. I was just the flower girls' aunt, and perfectly content with my lack of responsibility.

Both Katie and Megan had "independent personalities." That's how my sister described them.

"Ornery," my father said. "They take after their mother."

The girls looked lovely dressed in identical lacy white dresses and white patent shoes, their matching towheads neatly combed. That was before we left my sister's house.

The drive to the church took almost an hour through freeway traffic. I was squeezed in back between the girls' two car seats, Rosemary and her husband in front. Three adults to two children seemed decent odds to manage the journey.

By the time we got to the church, the dry autumn air had turned my nieces' wispy hair into electric straw, Katie's sash had pulled loose, and Megan's white anklets had dropped into her now scuffed shoes. How had she scuffed her shoes riding in a car?

We took them into the church nursery to repair the damage and waited for the rest of the wedding party to arrive. There were toys in the nursery. The girls had all the games and dolls and books on the floor within minutes. Megan latched onto a naked baby doll with hair as fly-away as her own.

"Baby doesn't have any clothes," Megan said. She found a ratty black crocheted poncho in the toy box to tuck around the doll. "Now she's got a blankie!"

We managed to entertain the girls until time to queue up in back of the church. Megan took the baby doll wrapped in its black blankie along with her white basket of flowers. After some last minute primping to slick down their hair, pull up their socks, and re-tie their sashes, we left them with one of the bridesmaids and followed the ushers to our pew.

The music started. The flower girls walked in side by side. Katie solemnly scattered her flowers as she had been instructed at the rehearsal. Megan stomped along, carrying her flower basket in one hand. In the other, she clutched the naked doll, bare bottom up and black poncho trailing.

Megan stopped beside her mother in the second pew.

"Go on," Rosemary whispered between clenched teeth, pushing Megan on toward the altar with Katie.

But Megan would have none of it, her lower lip stuck forward in a pout. Snickers arose from those who witnessed the quiet drama between mother and daughter.

Rosemary gave up and pulled Megan and the baby doll into the pew beside her.

Katie continued up the aisle by herself.

The adults processed and the ceremony progressed – songs, readings, vows, and more songs. About halfway through, Katie decided she was tired, and plopped down on the top step to the altar, legs sprawled in front of her. After the last reading, she let out a loud sigh, audible in the back of the church. More snickers from the congregation.

At the end of the service, the bride and groom marched out to joyful music, the bridesmaids and groomsmen following.

And Katie still sat on the altar step, looking very confused.

Apparently, she had not received instruction during the rehearsal on when to leave. The kindly minister took her hand and they walked out together, passing Rosemary, Megan, and baby doll.

Katie grinned at her sister. Megan pouted back.

Thankfully, that was the last wedding of my generation. The next close relatives in my family to be married are likely to be my son and daughter. I don't know if we'll have any children of appropriate age to be ring bearer and flower girl, but I'm hoping not.

I've already told my daughter I'd pay her to elope.

# YOGURT AND APPLESAUCE

When my children were little, I wanted meals to be fast and easy. And healthy.

Weekend lunches were a challenge, because there wasn't always fast, easy, healthy food in the house. It depended on whether I'd made it to the grocery store in the last few days.

I tried to keep things like cottage cheese and yogurt and fruit on hand to go with sandwiches. I must have done an adequate job, because our house had the reputation in the neighborhood of being where the kids only got healthy snacks. We didn't have too many lunch time visitors.

"Joel's mom gives us potato chips," my son told me. He liked to go to Joel's house around noon on Saturdays.

My kids were not very picky, but they didn't like plain yogurt and preferred the brand with fruit on the bottom. And they refused to eat plain cottage cheese. So to get these foods down them, I had to be creative.

If I only had cottage cheese or plain yogurt, I added my own fruit. I put in whatever canned fruit I had on hand. Sometimes I ran out of canned fruit, too. Then I'd move on to applesauce. I usually had applesauce; the jars were large enough I could get to the store for more before it was used up.

My kids seemed to relish mixing their cottage cheese and apple-sauce. It looked disgusting, but actually didn't taste bad.

One day I had no cottage cheese. So I gave them yogurt. Of course, it needed something, so I spooned applesauce on top of the yogurt. It looked disgusting, too, but I slapped the plates in front of the kids.

"Here's lunch," I said.

And that is how yogurt and applesauce became the favorite snack in our household.

I made Joel eat it, too, when he visited.

### # # #

Just mix approximately equal portions of yogurt and applesauce. Any flavor of yogurt will do, but peach is particularly good.

Or put the yogurt and applesauce side by side on the plate and let the kids do the mixing. They'll probably eat more if they participate in meal preparation.

# PARTLY MINE

His tiny fingers wrap around my thumb,
fragile, yet determined,
holding tight, even in sleep.
His grip is all yours.

At least his hair is straight like mine.

# DRESS CODE

When she was five, I begged my daughter, "Wear
the pretty pinafore, it looks so sweet."
She shook her head and told me, "Teacher says
not to wear a dress on monkey bars."

When she was fifteen, "Cover up," I yelled,
"Don't hike your skirt, and wash that make-up off."
But she ignored my orders and commands
and followed fashions of her teen-age peers.

Now she's twenty-five, and all I crave
is one approving word about my clothes.
"Those jeans fit well, Mom," signifies she cares
more than any sappy greeting card.

# MEETING OF THE MINDS

During one of my attempts to be a better parent, I decided we should have family meetings. My kids were at or near their teenage years, and the parenting books said they should have a voice in family decisions. Meetings at work seemed to make things happen; why not at home?

I scheduled the first session with husband and kids and prepared my agenda – chore assignments, school events, and vacation plans.

"Can I put something on the agenda?" my fifteen-year-old son Jamie asked when we gathered in the family room at the appointed time one spring evening.

That wasn't in the plan. But I supposed his request was reasonable; at least I couldn't think of a reason to object. The point, after all, was to give the kids a voice. "Okay," I said.

"I want to talk about getting a dog."

My heart sank. Already the meeting had derailed.

Our dog Rickover had died two years earlier at the ripe old age of fourteen. The past two years had been blissful, in my opinion. No more arguments over whose turn it was to clean up the back yard. We could leave for the weekend without worrying about who would feed the dog. We had just redecorated the house with new white carpet.

But Jamie was firm. He wanted another dog. It was the first thing I had seen him enthusiastic about since he turned thirteen, other than the Kansas City Chiefs.

"I think getting a new dog is a good idea," my husband said.

"Two dogs," twelve-year-old Marcy piped up. "Aunt Nancy has two dogs, and she says they play with each other and don't need as much attention. Besides, that way Jamie and I each get to pick one. He shouldn't get to choose."

I was outvoted. If all three of them were lined up against me, we would get a dog. Maybe two.

A couple of Saturdays later found us at the animal shelter. I was silent, but inwardly fuming. The rest of the family was excited.

All the puppies were adorable. Of course. That's what puppies do – eat, poop, and act adorable.

One kennel held three litter mates labeled as "Lab mixes." Their paws were huge.

"How big are these puppies going to get?" I asked the woman who showed us the dogs.

"Not too big," she said, shrugging. "Maybe forty pounds."

Rickover – a Lab mix – had been sixty pounds; seventy pounds in his heavy years, before the vet told us to put him on a diet. My husband Al, a Navy man, had complied with orders as if his pension depended on it. Rickover soon took to licking the floor for sustenance.

I could handle forty pounds.

We took the puppies into the yard so the kids could look at the three litter mates. It would be hard to take two of the dogs and leave one. Then one puppy licked Jamie's hand. "I want this one," he said.

One stepped on another. Marcy wanted the dog that had been squished by its sibling. She felt sorry for it.

The kids' decisions were final. We would be the proud owners of two female puppies. We paid the adoption and medical fees for the chosen two ($100 each) and arranged to return Tuesday evening after the dogs had been spayed to pick them up.

From the animal shelter, we went straight to the pet store to purchase food, dishes, leashes, toys and other basic dog needs. I think the tab was close to $500. One dog is expensive; two are an annual 401(k) contribution.

"We need names," I said, as we drove home from the pet store. That's when the real family discussion began.

"I want girl names," Marcy declared.

"I want nautical names," my husband said. "We had Rickover, and we should have Navy names again." (Admiral Hyman Rickover had started the Navy's nuclear submarine program, and my husband had named our first dog after the admiral he admired. As a result of the strange looks we got when people heard this story, I insisted on naming our kids when they came along.)

"Well, I think the names should match," I said. "Like twins, because that's what the puppies are." If we were going to have the dogs, we might as well name them something cute, I thought. "What do you want?" I asked Jamie.

"Nothing stupid." Now that he was about to get his dogs, Jamie was back to teenage indifference.

All weekend long we argued. No names suited everyone. The kids and I threw out all the nautical words we could think of (a list quickly exhausted). None of the Navy terms seemed like a good dog's name, and coming up with two was impossible. Marcy proposed all the girl names she liked. Jamie thought most of them were dumb.

On Monday night, Al declared, "We'll name them Lexington and Saratoga."

"Why?" I asked. Where was the naval significance in those names? Sounded like landlocked battlefields to me.

"They're aircraft carriers. Lexington class. The Saratoga was her sister ship. There was a third carrier in the class, too. Like the puppy we didn't take."

"And we can call them Lexi and Sara," Marcy said, excitement in her eyes.

"What do you think?" I asked Jamie.

He shrugged. "Okay." Must not be too stupid.

So we agreed, and Lexi and Sara were named.

Though our family was able to come to a meeting of the minds on the dogs' names, we hadn't had as good of luck in what we were told by the animal shelter. The woman at the shelter was wrong about how big they'd get. Lexi – the puppy who had been trampled – grew to sixty-five pounds and was the undisputed alpha dog. That Saturday when Marcy picked her out was the only time Lexi ever let her sibling get the best of her. Sara was fifty-five pounds and as sneaky as they came at avoiding anything she disliked, from pills to cameras to thunder.

Furthermore, the dogs were not "Lab mixes." We never really knew what they were, but we couldn't see any Labrador. Our vet said they were probably Irish wolfhound mix. They were certainly willing to hunt the wolves in our neighborhood – any dog not in their pack was fair game.

I only permitted a few more family meetings before that fad bit the dust. I didn't like the surprises that developed.

Thankfully, Lexi and Sara were the only permanent reminders of my folly. They lived to be old ladies – Lexi died at thirteen and Sara lived to be almost fifteen. When I retired, they happily moved from dog run into kitchen.

And I did my best to keep them off the white carpet.

## UNTIL THE ALARM SOUNDS

I am yours, for this brief moment
before the coffee perks,
before the paper comes,
before the day intrudes.

For now, we twine beneath the quilt,
and life is small and safe.

# FAMILY RECIPE

Angela sautéed onions and garlic, then stirred in sausage to brown. She dumped the mixture into a large stew pot and poured in cans of tomato sauce, tomato paste, canned tomatoes and tomato soup. Her mother had spent years tweaking this recipe, changing the blend of tomatoes until it matched the texture and taste of sauce made from scratch. Tomato soup had been the last ingredient added.

After dumping in the tomatoes, Angela chopped fresh spices. She could hear her mother say, "It's the spices that make the difference. Fresh basil and oregano." Angela's grandmother, born in Italy, refused to use any ingredients out of a can, but Angela's American-born mother decreed canned tomatoes were acceptable, if the spices were fresh. Angela followed her mother's rules; she always had.

The spaghetti sauce needed to simmer all day, and Angela rarely had time to make it. But today was Saturday, and Bob had the kids at swimming lessons. She reveled at being alone for the morning, even if she spent her time doing chores. The house was quiet, except for the kitchen exhaust fan sucking away the pungent sausage and onion odors. Despite the fan, the house always smelled like spaghetti for days after she made the sauce.

Outside the kitchen window, the sky dripped grey drizzle. Winter in Seattle; what did she expect? At least Seattle didn't have the cold lake winds she had grown up with in Chicago.

She remembered winter Sundays when her mother made spaghetti sauce. Every Sunday through high school, Angela helped her mother cook another boring family dinner for her older brothers and their families. They gathered for Sunday dinner in her parents' small house in the Near West Side of Chicago.

Angela's mother had been forty-one when Angela was born. Her brothers were fourteen, sixteen and eighteen years older. Angela was sure her conception had been an accident, though no one ever said so. Her parents had always seemed old to her, and her brothers had left home before she started grade school.

Angela yearned to leave Chicago when she went to college to escape her lonely childhood. But her father insisted she go to the University of Illinois at Chicago near their house. Her brothers had gone out of town to college, but she could not.

"Your mother needs your help," he said. "She isn't getting any younger."

Angela met Bob during college and married him right after graduation. He took a programming job with Microsoft, and they moved to Seattle. Now, eight years and two kids later, at age thirty, she was happy with the life she and Bob had built.

As she gave the pot a final stir, Angela shook her head and smiled. All that reminiscing prompted by the smell of spaghetti sauce. The sauce didn't require constant tending, and she needed to get on with other chores. She turned to leave the kitchen, but the ringing phone made her stop.

"Angela?" Her mother's voice quavered. "Angela, I don't know where I am."

"Mom? What do you mean you don't know where you are?"

"I got lost."

"What happened?" Angela rubbed her forehead and tried to speak calmly, keeping the pitch of her voice low. Since her father's death seven years ago, her mother had become increasingly confused. Sometimes talking to her was more difficult than talking to one of the children.

"I'm in a hotel room. But I don't know where."

"A hotel? What are you doing in a hotel?"

"It was night. I was lost. I had to sleep."

"Okay, Mom. Are you calling from the phone in your room?" The room phone should have an address.

"Yes." Her mother's voice still trembled.

"Mom, look on the phone. Does it have the hotel's name and address?"

"Yes."

"What does it say?" Angela felt like she was questioning her six-year-old.

"Hampton Inn. Some street in Naperville."

"Naperville? What are you doing out there?" Naperville was almost thirty miles from her mother's apartment on Cabrini Street in Chicago.

"I went to the drug store. I got lost."

"The drug store down the street? How could you go to the drug store and end up in Naperville?"

"I don't know," her mother wailed. Angela guessed there were tears streaming down her mother's cheeks.

"Mom, calm down. You need to calm down. Is your car there?"

"I think so. I must have parked it last night when I checked in."

"Okay. When you've calmed down, you can drive home. Then call me back, and we'll talk some more." Angela paused. "Why didn't you call one of the boys?" Even though her brothers were now in their forties, her mother still called them "the boys." They all lived near Chicago.

"I didn't want to bother them," her mother said, her voice barely audible.

So that's it, Angela thought. She's embarrassed. Doesn't want the boys to know. But she doesn't mind bothering me. It's still my job to help her.

"Can you get home, Mom?"

"I don't know."

"Do you want me to call one of the boys?"

"No, no. I'll get home."

"Are you sure?" Angela frowned.

"I can do it."

"I want you to call me when you get home."

"Which way do you think I should go?" her mother asked.

Angela sighed. Mom can't drive home, she decided. Half a continent away, Angela was helpless.

"Mom, I'm calling Frank. Don't go anywhere. I'll call you back after I talk to him. Give me the address and phone number for the hotel." Her mother read her the information off the telephone. "Mom, I'm hanging up now, but I'll call back."

She hung up and walked to the stove to give the spaghetti sauce a hard stir, psyching herself up to call Frank. When will the boys start helping without me asking? she wondered. She took a deep breath, and quickly punched her oldest brother's phone number into the handset. "Frank, it's Angela. Mom got lost last night. She's in Naperville."

"What?" Her brother's voice boomed over the line. "I talked to her just before dinner yesterday. What happened?"

"She says she went to the drug store and got lost. You have to go get her. I don't think she can get herself home."

"I've got a tee time in thirty minutes."

"Well, I can't get there from Seattle in thirty minutes. You'll have to do it or get one of the other boys to go."

"Angela, I told you at Christmas we needed to make some plans for Mom. She's getting to the point where she can't live by herself."

"You know she'd hate giving up her own place."

"She got used to the apartment we got her after Dad died. You didn't think she could do that. The other boys and I have our own lives. We can't keep dropping everything to deal with her. You're in Seattle. You can't do anything. Moving her is our decision."

"I'm the one she called, Frank. We can't argue about moving her now. You've got to get her."

Frank sighed. "Where is she?"

"Hampton Inn in Naperville. I told her to stay there. Her car's probably there, too, so it'd be best if you take Gina to drive Mom's car back."

There was a long silence. Then Frank said, "So now I have to drag my wife into this, too?"

"She's in it whether she likes it or not. Just get Mom, then call me." Angela gave Frank the Hampton Inn address and phone number, and hung up.

She called her mother, going through the hotel switchboard. "Mom, Frank's on his way. Don't go anywhere. He'll find you and drive you home."

"Now, why'd you go and bother Frank? You know how busy he is. I could have driven home."

"I told you, Mom. You can't; you're lost. Let's just chat until Frank gets there." Angela knew it would take her brother at least thirty minutes to drive to Naperville from his home in Evanston. She hoped he would hurry. In the meantime, she would chat with her mother to keep her at the hotel. She hadn't planned to spend the morning in the kitchen, but it was all she could do to help her mother at the moment.

Angela moved a stool next to the stove and sat. The sauce didn't need her attention, but she stirred it for something to do. "I'm making your spaghetti sauce," she said. "Fresh basil and oregano, just like you always said." She sniffed the savory spices and smiled.

# ITALIAN SPAGHETTI SAUCE

**INGREDIENTS:**
 ½ cup of olive oil
 1 ½ cup onions, finely chopped
 4 cloves garlic, finely chopped
 3 lbs ground beef
 ½ lb hot Italian sausage, ground or in small pieces
 12 oz tomato paste
 1 can tomato soup
 2 cups water
 29 oz canned tomatoes (1 large can)
 29 oz tomato sauce
 1 ½ tsp Worcestershire sauce
 1 tsp salt
 1 tsp sugar
 ½ tsp celery salt
 3 bay leaves
 1 dash cinnamon
 1 dash oregano
 4 whole allspice, crushed
 ½ lb fresh mushrooms or 1 small can (4 ½ oz)
 1 can sliced olives (4 oz)

## DIRECTIONS:

1. Heat olive oil in heavy skillet. Cook onion and garlic till onion is tender. Add beef and sausage and brown well.
2. Combine remaining ingredients, except mushrooms and olives, in large heavy pot. Stir in meats and onion and garlic.
3. Bring mixture to boiling and simmer, uncovered, at least 4 hours, stirring occasionally. Do not let mixture stick to bottom of pot. (Can be cooked in crock pot for 8-10 hours.)
4. 30 minutes before sauce is done, stir in mushrooms and olives.
5. Serve over cooked pasta with grated Parmesan cheese. Makes enough for 8-12 generous servings.

## NOTES:

- Although this is the recipe I had in mind while writing the story, *Family Recipe*, I use all dried herbs. No need for fresh. You can substitute other kinds of sausage, and increase or decrease the meats to suit your taste.
- This recipe can be doubled, if you have a big enough pot. I've fed a whole cross-country team on a doubled recipe.
- Freezes well.
- Sauce stains terribly. Do not wear new clothes while eating. Do not leave children unattended, unless you can hose them and the room off after they eat.

# ARACHNOPHOBIA AND LOVE

"If you want me to marry you, you have to promise to kill all the spiders," I demanded of my fiancé.

I have always been deathly afraid of spiders. One good reason to marry was to have someone to dispose of unwanted nasties. If he wouldn't make this promise, he wasn't the right man for me.

"You've got to be kidding," he responded.

"Seriously," I said. I wouldn't let it go. I nagged him till he agreed.

Of course, he's broken his commitment many times in our thirty-four years of marriage. He sometimes was away when the arachnids crept out. He was more worried about staining and denting walls and ceilings than about disposing of the critters efficiently. Over the years, he pursued his duties as spider assassin with indifference.

But I still considered it part of the marriage vows. And, to give him credit, he often abandoned his book or TV show – albeit with deep sighs of disgust at my fright – to exterminate the spiders.

Until a few months ago, when he broke his ankle and had surgery to mend it. In the middle of a Midwestern heat wave.

Something about temperatures above 85 degrees brings spiders out of our attic and into the rooms below. This summer, with temperatures exceeding 95 degrees for weeks on end, even the grand-daddy spiders left the security of the attic for the comfort of air-conditioning.

My husband's immobility meant I had to kill them. I didn't respond well to my new responsibility.

As disabilities go, we were very lucky. His ankle healed. But it gave me the opportunity to reflect on many aspects of disability and caregiving.

First, I discovered the instantaneous disruption that injuries and sudden illness can cause. Our schedule came to an abrupt halt with his accident, and was further disturbed after the surgery. I became valet, cook and chauffeur, in addition to spider slayer, with no warning. We had to cancel two vacations, one of which was a long-anticipated trip to a remote wilderness – impossible when he could not walk.

I also learned about my lack of patience. I was easily frustrated by minor inconveniences, even though I loved the man making demands on me. I wondered as I toted and fetched for him, trotting up and down the stairs more times than I thought possible, if he couldn't do a little more for himself – at least put on his own sock, for goodness sake. If his injury really required all the moaning and groaning and constant twitching at night. If he had to give me detailed instructions on how to water the yard and clean the kitchen and take over all the other chores he had done for years. And if he couldn't phrase his requests for help with just a little more gratitude and a little less entitlement.

When I was on crutches many years ago, I said "thank you" so many times to so many people every day. I learned that people were very willing to help, but it was important to show my appreciation. Why couldn't my husband learn the same lesson? Especially when I reminded him.

In addition, I was humbled when I compared myself to the couples I know who have faced huge health crises in their marriages. My father has adapted to my mother's dementia. My mother-in-law has coped for years with my father-in-law's blindness and increasing immobility. Even after his move to a nursing home, she visits him almost every day. A friend has handled her husband's care since his stroke over two years ago; he is still in rehabilitation, which may last the rest of his life.

These caregivers face long-term debilitating health issues with courage, endurance, and generally good humor. They must feel the emotions I felt magnified a thousand times – irritation at demands from those who cannot help themselves, resentment at the disruption to their lives, fear of confronting new responsibilities. Yet they continued to provide care. Because what other option did they have?

Finally, I learned the importance of caring for one's self along with the loved one in need. One day shortly after my husband's surgery I volunteered all day in a customer service role, and then came home to take care of him. I was frazzled. Before I could cook his dinner I needed solitude and silence. I left him alone for another half-hour while I read the newspaper.

I told my husband what I was doing, and he said, "So you're putting your oxygen mask on first."

"What do you mean?" I asked.

"The flight attendants say to put on your mask before helping your child. Is that what you're doing?"

He was right – that's what I was doing. And it was important. Caregivers face responsibilities that seem endless, which is why it is vital to have interests and escapes apart from caregiving.

So I learned a lot while he was laid up. I am sorry my husband was in pain, but I'm glad I had the opportunity to reflect about caregiving.

But I'm not glad I had to deal with spiders. I will never make that adjustment, no matter what the future brings.

# ABOUT THE AUTHOR

Theresa Hupp is an award winning author from Kansas City. She was a Midwest Voices columnist with **THE KANSAS CITY STAR** in 2010, and has worked with *Kansas City Voices* literary magazine and its publisher, Whispering Prairie Press, in several capacities, including Assistant Prose Editor, Secretary, Treasurer, and President. Theresa is a member of the Kansas City Writers Group, Oklahoma Writers Federation Inc., and Write Brain Trust.

If you enjoyed these stories, please contact Theresa at mthupp@gmail.com or follow her blog at http://mthupp.wordpress.com.

www.ingramcontent.com/pod-product-compliance
Lightning Source LLC
Chambersburg PA
CBHW071223130626
46555CB00004B/1813